In the world of *Sweet Pickles,* each animal gets into a pickle because of an all too human personality trait.

This book is about Clever Camel. She's very practical and can fix anything, including Kidding Kangaroo.

Other Books in the Sweet Pickles Series

ME TOO IGUANA
STORK SPILLS THE BEANS
ZEBRA ZIPS BY
GOOSE GOOFS OFF
VERY WORRIED WALRUS

Library of Congress Cataloging in Publication Data

Reinach, Jacquelyn.
Fixed by camel.

(Sweet Pickles series)
SUMMARY: Camel finds a practical way to handle an interfering Kangaroo.
[1. Camels–Fiction] I. Hefter, Richard. II. Title.
III. Series.
PZ7.R2747Fi [E] 76-43091
ISBN 0-03-01809-

Published simultaneously in Canada by Holt, Rinehart and Winston of Canada, Limited.

Printed in the United States of America

Weekly Reader Books' Edition

VROOM!
I'LL DO IT TOMORROW.
I FEEL FINE.
ME TOO.
I WANT. I WANT. I WANT. I WANT.
FEARLESS FISH
GOOF-OFF GOOSE
HEALTHY HIPPO
IMITATING IGUANA
JEALOUS JACKAL
YES!
?
BUSY, BUSY, BUSY.
I KNOW EVERYTHING.
I'LL HOLD MY BREATH!
POSITIVE PIG
QUESTIONING QUAIL
RESPONSIBLE RABBIT
SMARTY STORK
TEMPER TANTRUM TURTLE
YAK, YAK, YAK, YAK.
I DO IT MY WAY!
YAKETY YAK
ZANY ZEBRA
HERE THEY ARE
SWEET PICKLES®
All twenty-six of them
in stories with giggles
and tickles and awful pickles

Weekly Reader Books presents

FIXED BY CAMEL

Written by Jacquelyn Reinach
Illustrated by Richard Hefter
Edited by Ruth Lerner Perle

Holt, Rinehart and Winston · New York

One morning, Camel was fixing a pipe under Main Street when Kangaroo came along and slammed the cover shut over the manhole.

"Hey! What do you think you're doing?" cried Camel.

"I'm only kidding," giggled Kangaroo. "Haw, haw!"

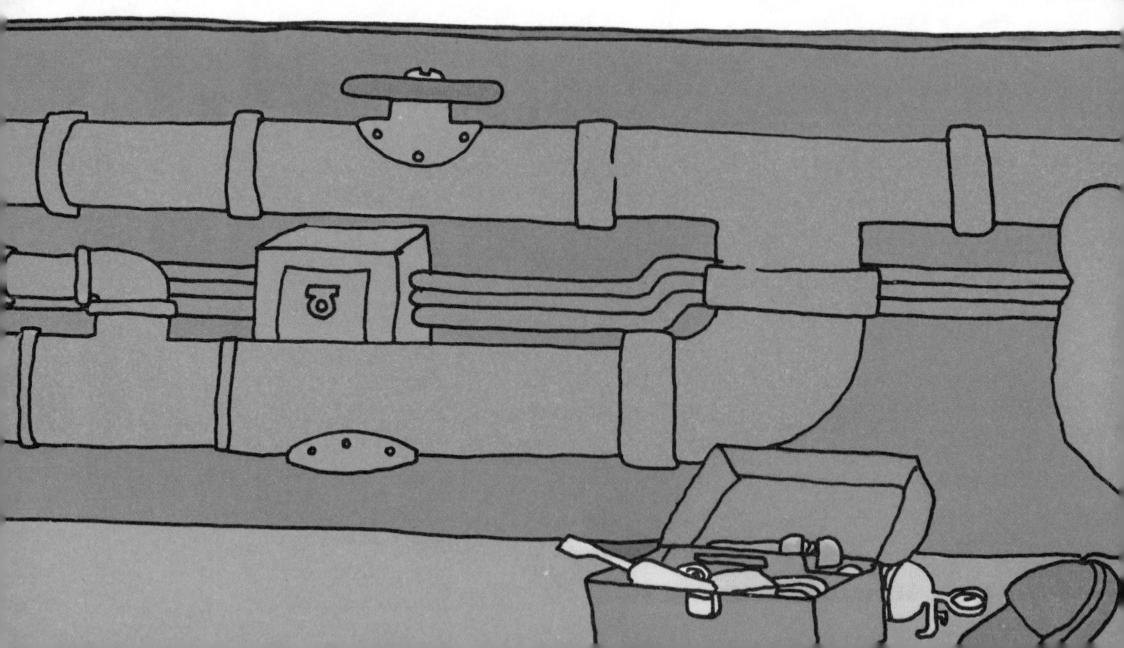

"Fine," said Camel, "then open the cover so I can get out."

"You're a clever Camel," called Kangaroo. "Do it yourself." Kangaroo sat down on the curb and howled with delight.

"VERRY funny," muttered Camel.

But Camel *was* clever. She could fix just about anything.

Camel thought a moment. Then she filled a big balloon with helium and let it go.

WOOSH! Up went the balloon. Off went the cover. Out came Camel.

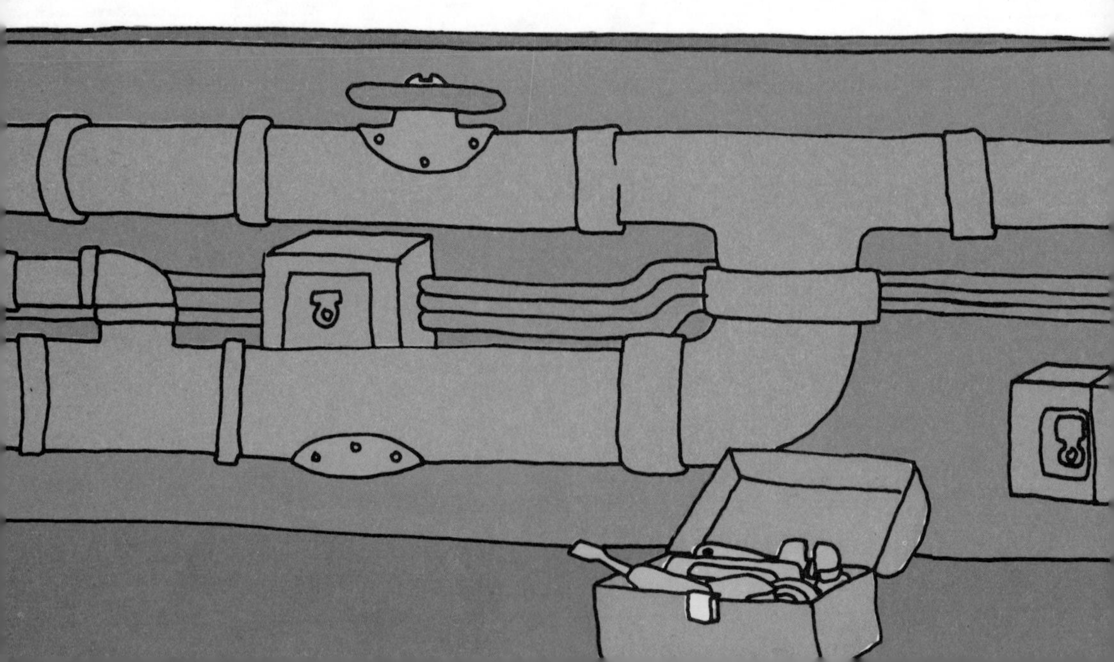

FIXED
BY
CAMEL
HELIUM

Kangaroo hopped over and gave Camel a hearty thump. "I knew you could do it, Camel," he said.

Camel didn't answer.

"You're not angry, are you?" asked Kangaroo. "I was only kidding! Haw, haw!"

"VERRY funny," said Camel and went off to work.

Camel was up on a roof banging a broken shingle when Kangaroo came along and took the ladder away.

"Hey! What do you think you're doing?" yelled Camel.

"I'm only kidding," chortled Kangaroo. "Haw, haw!"

"Fine," said Camel, "then put the ladder back."

"Then it wouldn't be funny anymore," said Kangaroo. "Anyway, can't you think of a way down? You can fix anything."

FIXED
BY
CAMEL
TRAVEL

"VERRY funny," said Camel. She took out a rope, tied it around the chimney and slid down.

"Bravo!" clapped Kangaroo.

"VERRY funny," said Camel again and went off to work.

Camel was mixing cement for a hole in the sidewalk when she saw Kangaroo peeking around the corner.

"Hmmmmm," she thought. "The minute I spread this wet cement, Kangaroo is sure to stick his feet in it. His kidding has got to stop!"

Then Camel said in a very loud voice, "Oh dear, I forgot a special job I must do in the park. I'll pour the cement for this sidewalk later."

CEMENT

Camel went off to the park.

Kangaroo followed.

First, Camel painted three park benches. She put up signs-WET PAINT, DO NOT TOUCH-and hid behind a tree.

Kangaroo came hopping along and began to scratch his name in the wet paint.

"Good!" thought Camel. "That will keep him busy for a while."

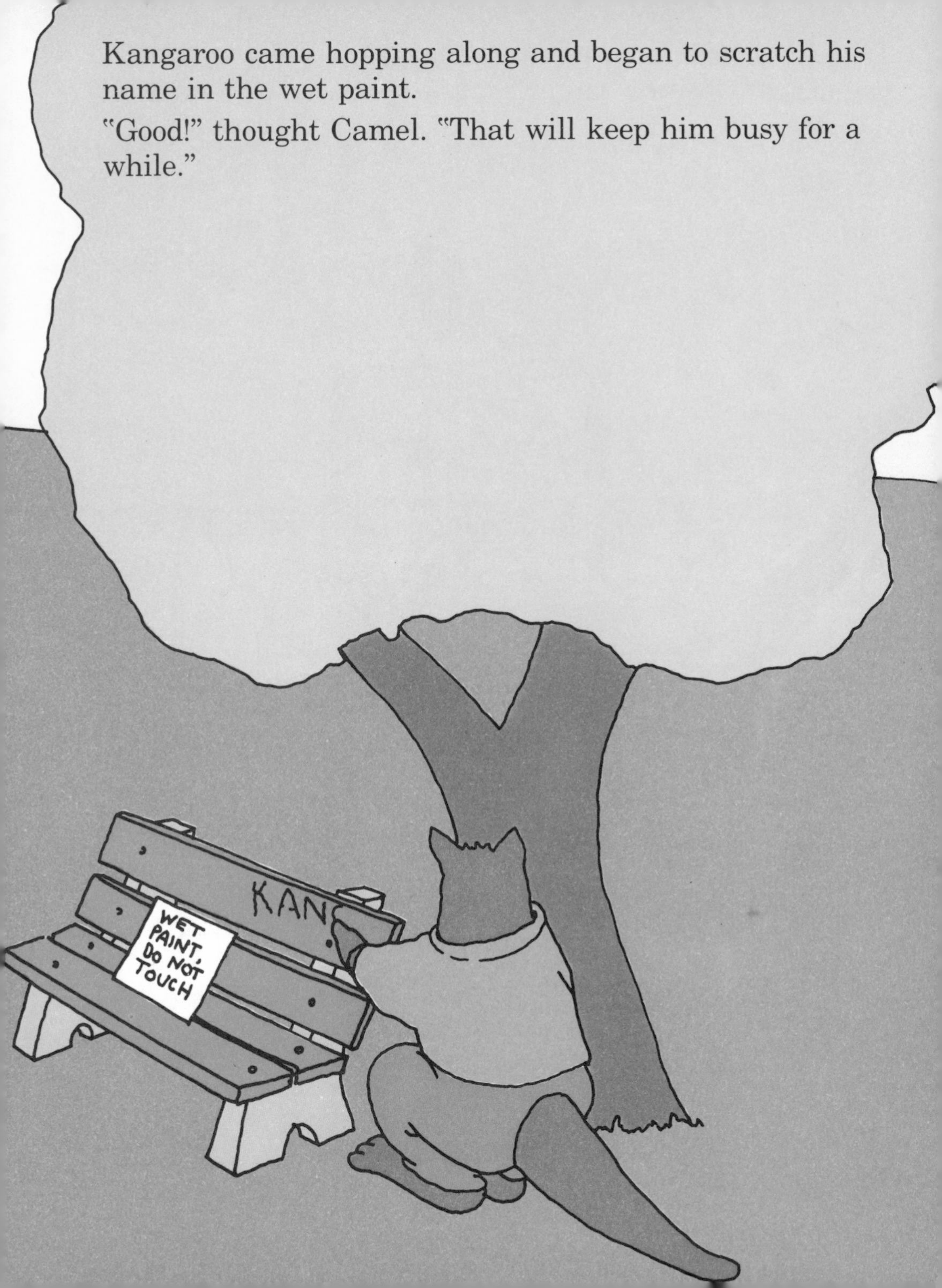

Then Camel hurried over to the playground. She knitted a net, draped it over a tall pole and stuck it in the middle of the jungle gym.

Then she took out some motors and gears and extension cords and ran back and forth between the jungle gym and the drinking fountain.

Then she tied a doorbell to the pole and nailed up a large sign-

DANGER!
DO NOT RING DOORBELL
UNDER ANY CIRCUMSTANCES

Finally, she put two peanut butter sandwiches and a quart of milk inside the jungle gym and sat down to wait.

Kangaroo came bounding into the playground. "Oh, there you are!" he called to Camel. "What're you fixing now?"

"I'm resting," said Camel. "I had a special job to finish."

"Oh, goody!" Kangaroo cried with delight. "A danger sign! Haw, haw!"

"I wouldn't go near that if I were you," said Camel.

DANGER!
DO NOT
RING

Kangaroo climbed up to have a closer look.

"Whatever you do, don't ring that bell," warned Camel.

"Haw, haw!" laughed Kangaroo. He pressed the button as hard as he could.

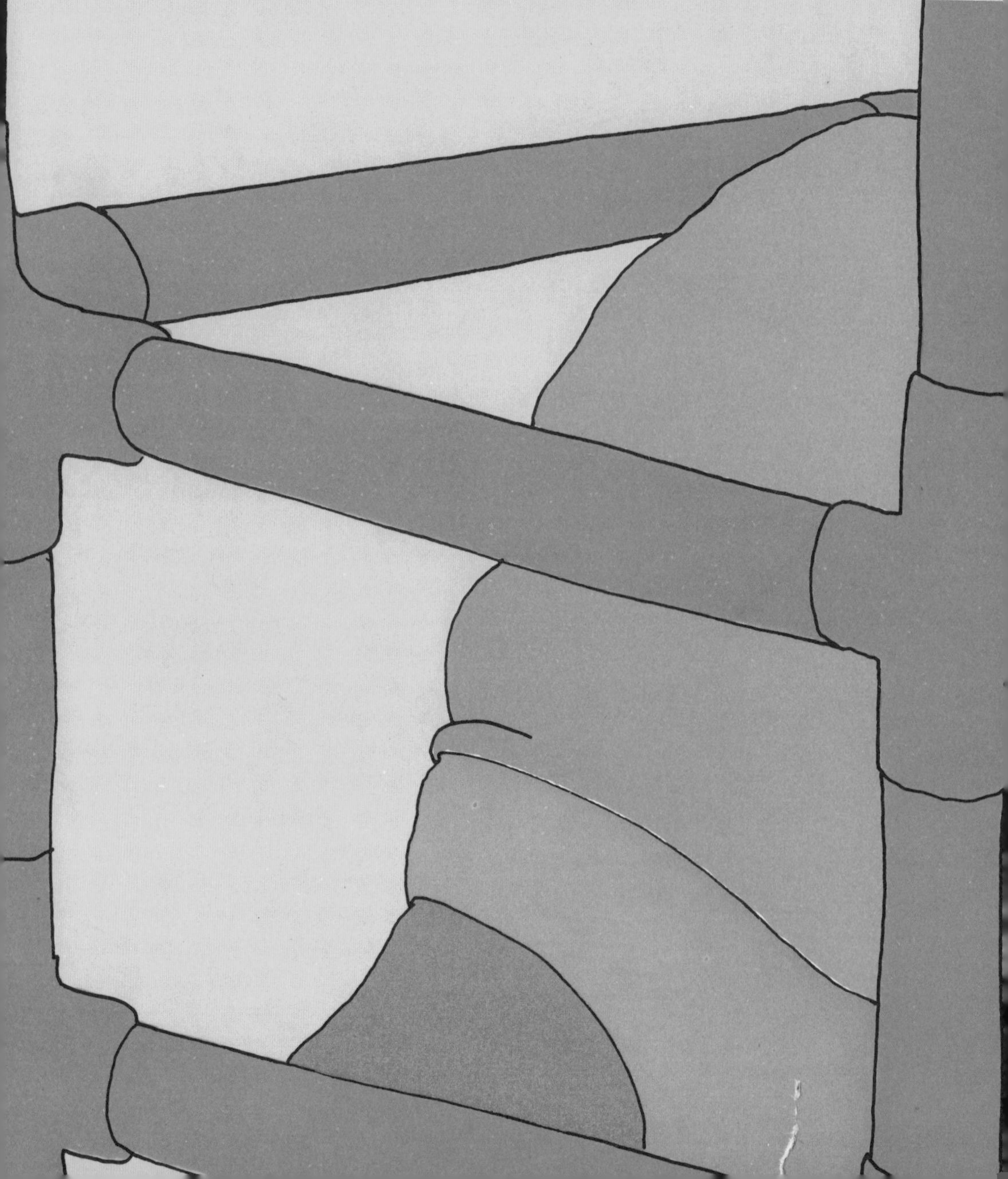

DANG
ER!
NOT
ELL
DER
ANY

WOOOOOOOOOOOOOOSH!

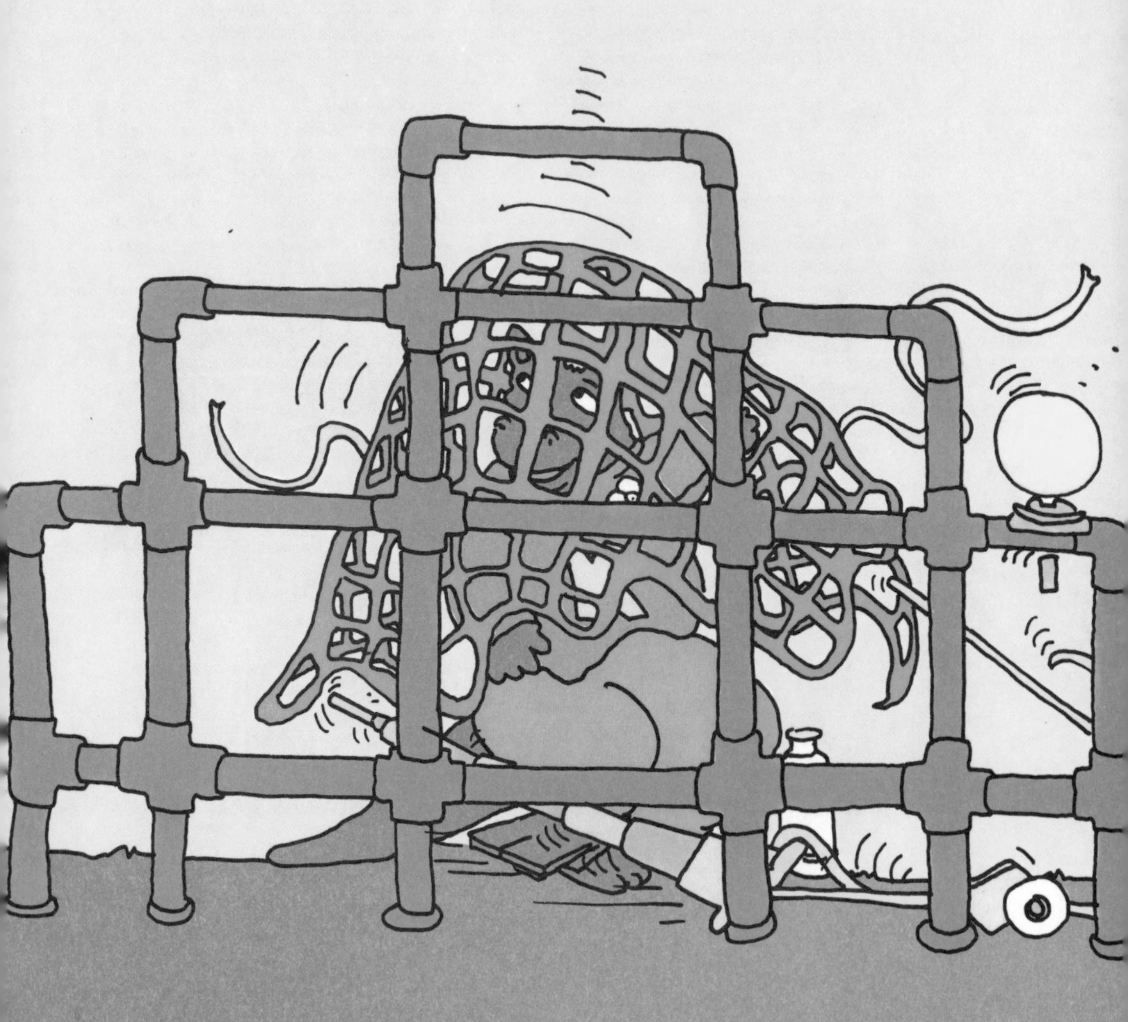

"Hey!" yelled Kangaroo. "What kind of joke is this?"

"A practical one," said Camel calmly. "Have a snack. I'll see you later... when the cement on my sidewalk is dry."